If You Were a Panda Bear

Panda Bear

Wendell and Florence Minor

KATHERINE TEGEN BOOKS
An Imprint of HarperCollins Publishers

If you were a panda bear,
Guess what you would wear?

A black-and-white suit
And eye patches—how cute!

You'd be very shy,
You'd eat lots of bamboo.

Then you'd take a long nap—
What a good thing to do!

If **you** were a sloth bear,
With long claws and strange hair,

Friends might think you looked funny,
But you wouldn't care!

You could peek through the ice.
See any seals? Who knows!

If **you** were a black bear,
You'd love to climb trees. . . .

You'd watch your cubs nip and bite,
And say, "Play nicely, please!"

If **you** were a **moon bear**,
You'd stay out late at night,

And the mark on your chest
Would look just like a light.

If you were a sun bear,
You'd have a
loooooooong tongue

To help you get honey.
Be careful—don't get stung!

If **you** were a grizzly bear,
You'd stand **tall** as ten feet.

You'd love catching salmon
With your paws and your teeth.

If **you** were a spectacled bear,
You'd have furry eyeglasses.

And if you went to school,
You'd look smart in your classes!

But if **you** were a teddy bear,
That might be the best.

What a cozy life you'd have
In your teddy bear nest!

Bear Fun Facts

 Giant Panda

- Newborn panda cubs weigh between 3 and 5 ounces and are only 6 inches long.

- Pandas spend two-thirds of their day eating and the rest of their day resting or sleeping.

- Pandas can eat 25 to 45 pounds of bamboo daily.

Sloth Bear

- Because of their long claws, sloth bears look clumsy walking on the ground, but they are agile tree climbers and can hang upside down by their claws.

- Termites are sloth bears' favorite food, but these bears also eat ants and bees. They sniff out their food with their long snouts, and a gap between their teeth lets them suck up the insects.

Polar Bear

- Even though polar bears look white, their hair is really made of clear, hollow tubes that reflect light. The color of a polar bear's coat can vary from pure white to shades of yellow.

- Polar bears can swim 100 miles or more without resting. They paddle through the water with their front paws and use their back legs to steer.

- A male polar bear can weigh between 800 and 1,600 pounds and can eat 10 percent of his body weight in half an hour, which means that a 1,000-pound bear could eat 100 pounds of food in that time.

American Black Bear

- American black bears usually have black coats, but their coats can also be cinnamon, blond, or honey colored.

- Black bears will eat almost anything, and like most bears, they are fond of honey. They often cause much damage when they break into beekeepers' hives to get at the honey.

Moon Bear (Asiatic Black Bear)

- The name "moon bear" comes from the mark on this bear's chest that looks like a crescent moon.

- These bears communicate in many different ways, including making clucking sounds when they play and "tut-tut-tut" sounds as a warning.

- Moon bears have been known to walk up to a quarter of a mile on their back legs.

Sun Bear

- Folklore says that the sun bear got its name from the golden or white patch on its chest, which represents the rising sun.

- Sun bears, smallest of the world's eight bear species, have 4-inch-long claws, which help them climb high up in trees, where they like to make their homes.

- An 8-to-10-inch-long, narrow tongue helps sun bears scoop out honey and grubs from beehives.

Grizzly Bear

- Grizzlies have been known to run at 30 miles an hour.

- As grizzlies prepare for winter hibernation, they can eat 90 pounds of food a day.

- The average height of a grizzly bear standing on its hind legs is about 7 feet, but they have been known to stand as tall as 10 feet.

Spectacled Bear (Andean Bear)

- Spectacled bears are also called Andean bears. They are the only bears found in South America. Since Paddington Bear of the well-known book series came from Peru in South America, he is a spectacled bear.

- A spectacled bear mother can carry a cub on her back or hold it to her chest with one front paw as she runs on three legs.

- Spectacled bears build leafy platforms in trees, which they use as feeding stations or sleeping areas. They have been known to sit in a tree for days, waiting for fruit to ripen.

Bear Sources and Websites

Bears of the World
• by Terry Domico, photographs by Terry Domico and Mark Newman (New York: Facts on File, 1988).

San Diego Zoo
• www.sandiegozoo.org/animalbytes/a-mammal.html

Polar Bears International
• www.polarbearsinternational.org/polar-bears/bear-essentials-polar-style/characteristics/fur-and-skin

Great Bear Foundation
• http://greatbear.org

Smithsonian National Zoo
• http://nationalzoo.si.edu/Publications/ZooGoer/1999/2/bearfacts.cfm

National Geographic
• http://kids.nationalgeographic.com/kids/animals/creaturefeature
• http://animals.nationalgeographic.com/animals/facts/?source=NavAniFact

Also by Wendell and Florence Minor

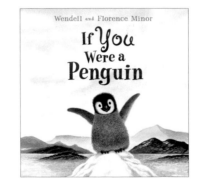

Wendell and Florence Minor

If You Were a Penguin

To the memory of my treasured friend Jean Craighead George,
who was an inspiration to me and whose work will
continue to inspire generations to come,
and for Adrianna and Sydney with much love
—F.M.

To Halina
—W.M.

Library of Congress Cataloging-in-Publication Data is available. ISBN 978-0-06-195090-2 (trade bdg.)

Typography by Dana Fritts. 13 14 15 16 17 SCP 10 9 8 7 6 5 4 3 2 1 ❖ First Edition